My Very First Story Time

Little Red Riding Hood

Retold by Rachel Elliot
Illustrated by Sophie Rohrbach

Little Red
Riding Hood

Mother

Father

Grandmother

basket

axe

flowers

ear

eye

teeth

wolf

house

hood

tree

wood

LITTLE RED RIDING HOOD lived at the edge of a wild, wild wood. One morning, she filled a basket with delicious things to take to her grandmother.

"Stay on the path," warned her mother. "Wolves will be watching and waiting."

I'm not worried about wolves,
thought Little Red Riding Hood.

The flowers along the path were so beautiful, that
Little Red Riding Hood soon forgot her mother's words.
So tall were the stems and so bright were the blooms, that
Little Red Riding Hood did not see the twitchy tail of a wolf.

"Such delicious things I can see," he smiled sneakily,
peering into her basket.

"Go away you wicked wolf!" cried Little Red Riding Hood. "These things are for my grandmother. She is ill in bed."

Then I will gobble your grandmother up, thought the wolf.

Deeper and deeper into the wood ran Little Red Riding Hood,
past bluebells and bluebirds and beetles and butterflies.

Grumble rumble went the wolf's tummy
as he watched her, licking his lips.

The wolf, being very sly, took a short-cut to Grandmother's house. She was very surprised to see him.
"Help!" the old lady cried, jumping into a cupboard and pulling the door closed behind her.

"I am feeling hungrier and hungrier!" roared the wolf.
"And my tummy is getting rumblier and rumblier!"
He put on some of Grandmother's clothes, climbed
into her bed, and waited for Little Red Riding Hood.

Soon, Little Red Riding Hood reached her grandmother's house. "Hello, Grandmother," she called, pushing open the door.

The sly wolf lay very still. Kind Little Red Riding
Hood crept into the bedroom.

"Come closer, little one," squeaked the wolf.
Rumble rumble, grumbled the wolf's tummy.

"What big ears you have, Grandmother," said
Little Red Riding Hood, peering down at the wolf.
"All the better to hear you with," he replied.

Little Red Riding Hood took another step forward.

"What big eyes you have," she said.

"All the better to see you with," replied the wolf.

The wolf's tummy went rumble, rumble, rumble again, and a huge smile broke across his face as he licked his lips.

"What big teeth you have," gasped Little Red Riding Hood, taking a step back.

"All the better to eat you with!" the wolf roared, throwing off the covers and springing from the bed.

"Help!" cried Little Red Riding Hood, running out of the house and along the path into the wild, wild wood. "Come back here and be eaten!" shouted the wolf.

The wicked wolf chased Little Red Riding Hood all along
the winding path, past bluebells and bluebirds, beetles and
butterflies until . . .

"Father! Mother!" Little Red Riding Hood cried.
"The wolf is coming!"

Red Riding Hood's father didn't like the look of the wolf. The wolf didn't like the look of the axe. He forgot all about his rumbling, grumbling tummy and ran back into the wood as fast as his legs would carry him.

Little Red Riding Hood and her mother and father rushed to rescue Grandmother.

"You must always be watchful and wary in the wood," warned Little Red Riding Hood's mother and father.
"Wolves don't worry me!" said Red Riding Hood.

But she never wandered far from the path again.

Can you spot five differences between these two pictures?

Can you name everything from
Little Red Riding Hood's basket?

What else would you
give to Grandmother?